CATASTROPHE!

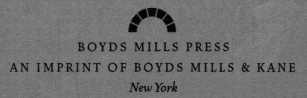

A STORY OF PATTERNS

Ann Marie Stephens

Illustrated by Jenn Harney

BOYDS MILLS PRESS

AN IMPRINT OF BOYDS MILLS & KANE

New York

The bait is packed and the boat is waiting.
This hungry crew wants to catch some dinner.

Line up along the lake!

Boots? Check.

Poles? Check.

Jackets?

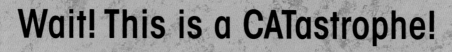

Wait! This is a CATastrophe!

Confused kitties cause lines to tangle.

We need a pattern.

Now change
and rearrange.

GREEN

ORANGE

GREEN

ORANGE

GREEN

Climb on into the canoe!

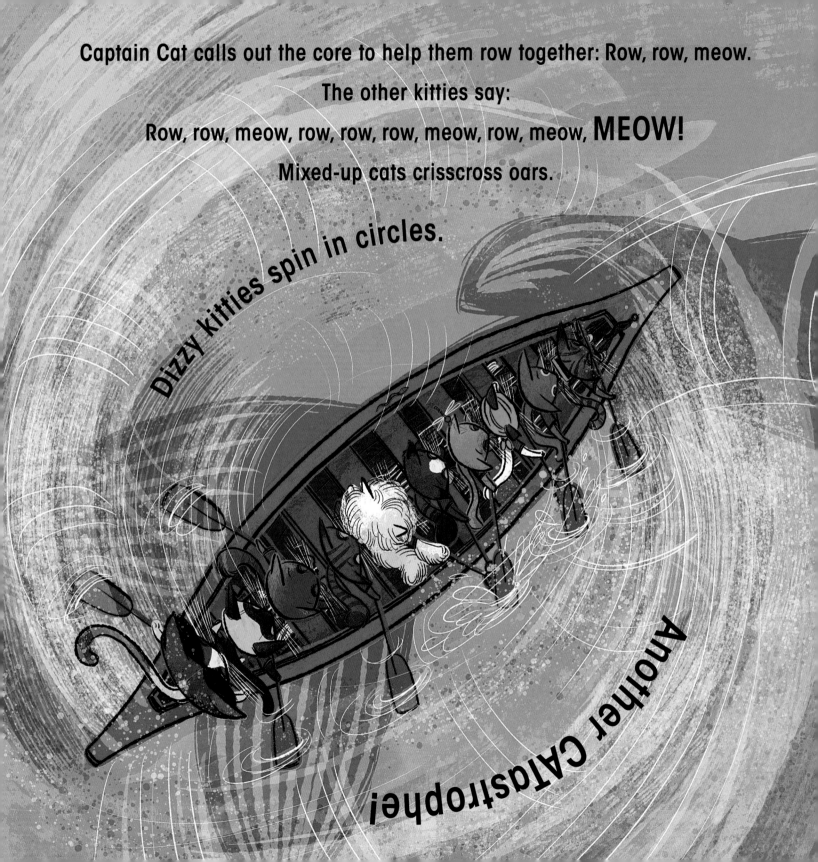

Captain Cat calls out the core to help them row together: Row, row, meow.

The other kitties say:

Row, row, meow, row, row, row, meow, row, meow, MEOW!

Mixed-up cats crisscross oars.

Dizzy kitties spin in circles.

Another CATastrophe!

Please repeat the core:

Row, row, meow, row, row, meow, row row, meow.

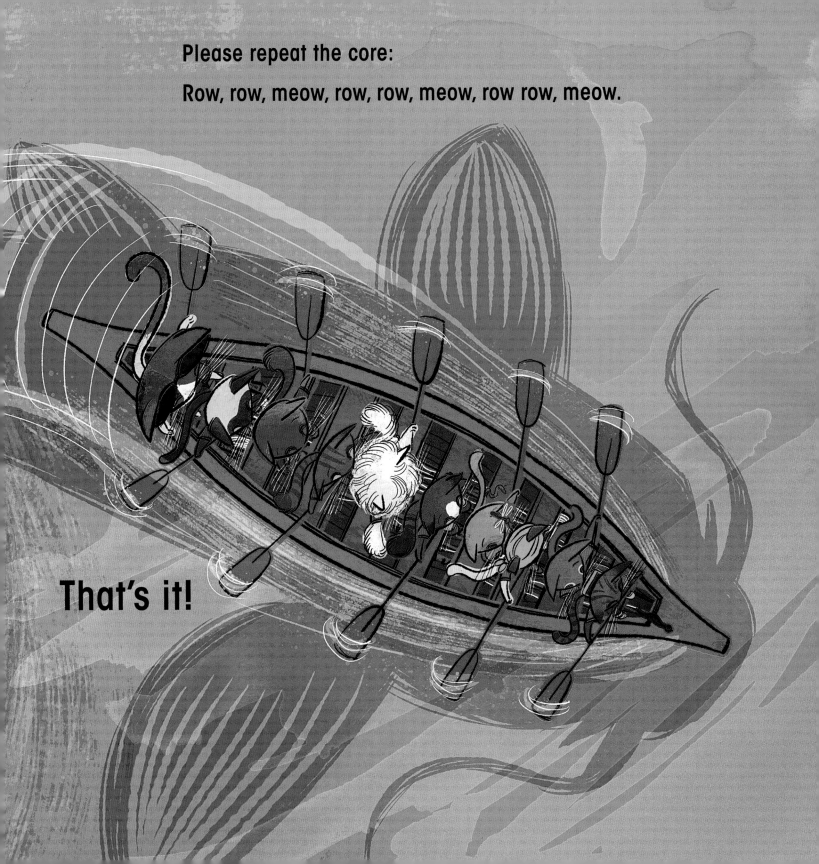

That's it!

Drop the anchor.
Down it goes.
Where it lands,
nobody knows . . .

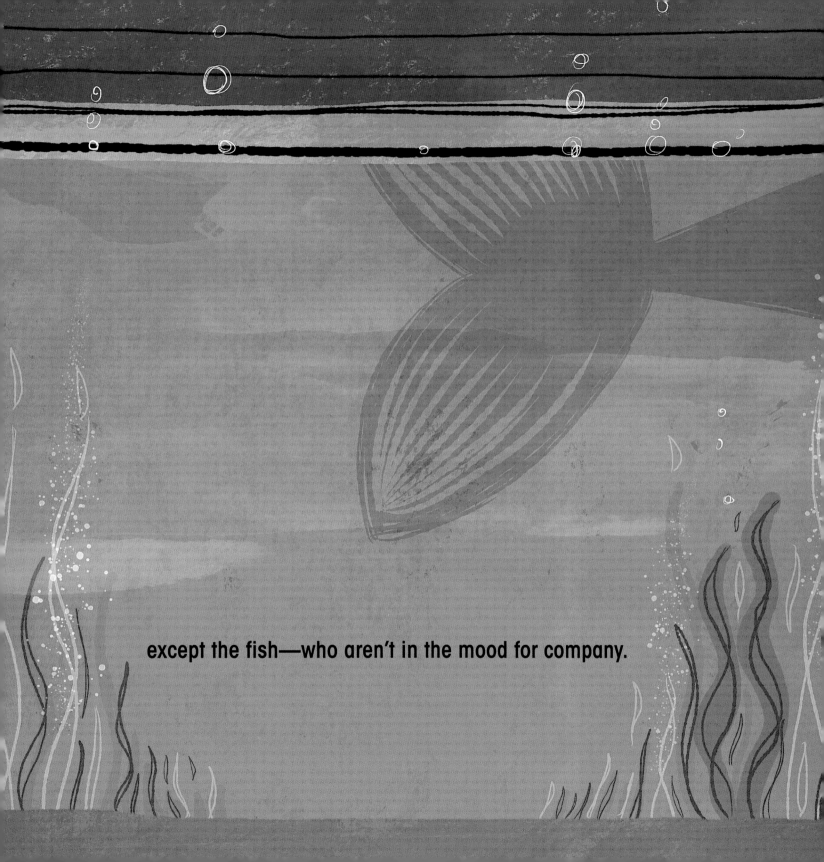

except the fish—who aren't in the mood for company.

The cats bait,
and the poles go in.

NEAR

FAR

MIDDLE

NEAR

FAR

MIDDLE

NEAR

FAR

MIDDLE

PLUNK!

OOPS!

Looks like the captain won't be catching anything today.

The cats wait for the fish to start biting. Fuzzy tails flick

Be careful kitties or the boat might tip.

We don't need another CATastrophe!

Try that pattern again.

The cats calm down while the fish finagle.

Suddenly, there's a flash and a tug.

It didn't take long for one fish to bite.

Captain Cat calls out the core:
Heave, heave, ho!

The other kitties repeat:

HEAVE, HEAVE, HO, HEAVE, HEAVE, HO, HEAVE, HEAVE, HO, HO—

WHOA!

This must be **the big one**

All paws on deck to help land this fish.
It's a tug-of-war!

BACK, FORTH, BACK, FORTH, BACK, FORTH, BACK, FORTH, BACK, BACK, BACK, BACK . . .

Watch out!

The boat is tipping.

The cats are flipping.

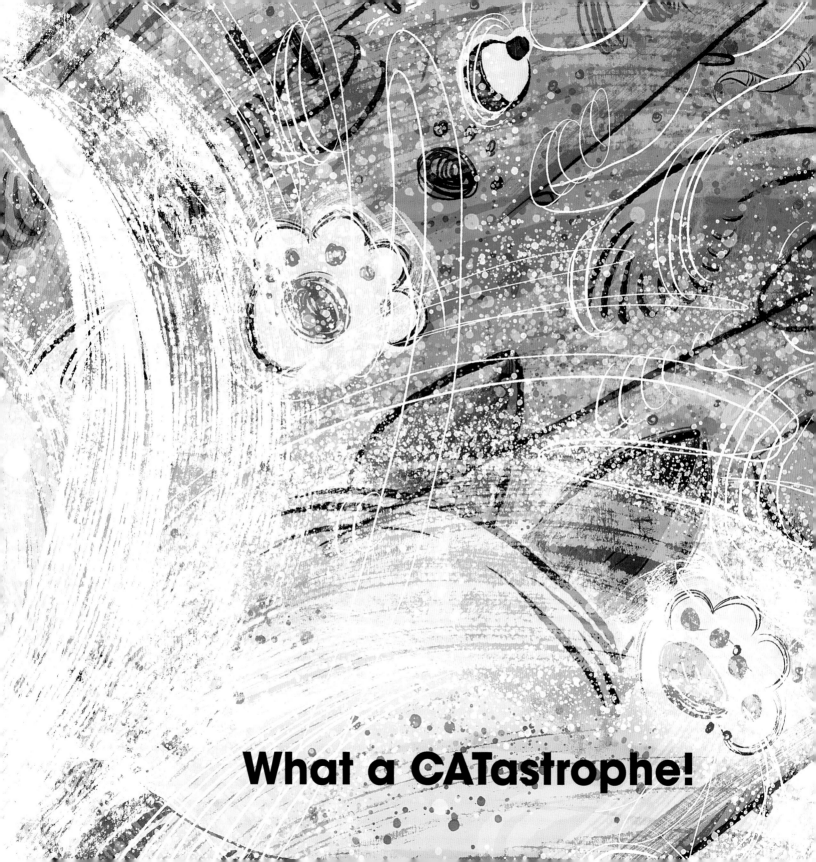

What a CATastrophe!

The captain guides the crew to shore,
by calling out the core:
PADDLE, KICK, MEOW.

The other kitties repeat:

PADDLE KICK MEOW

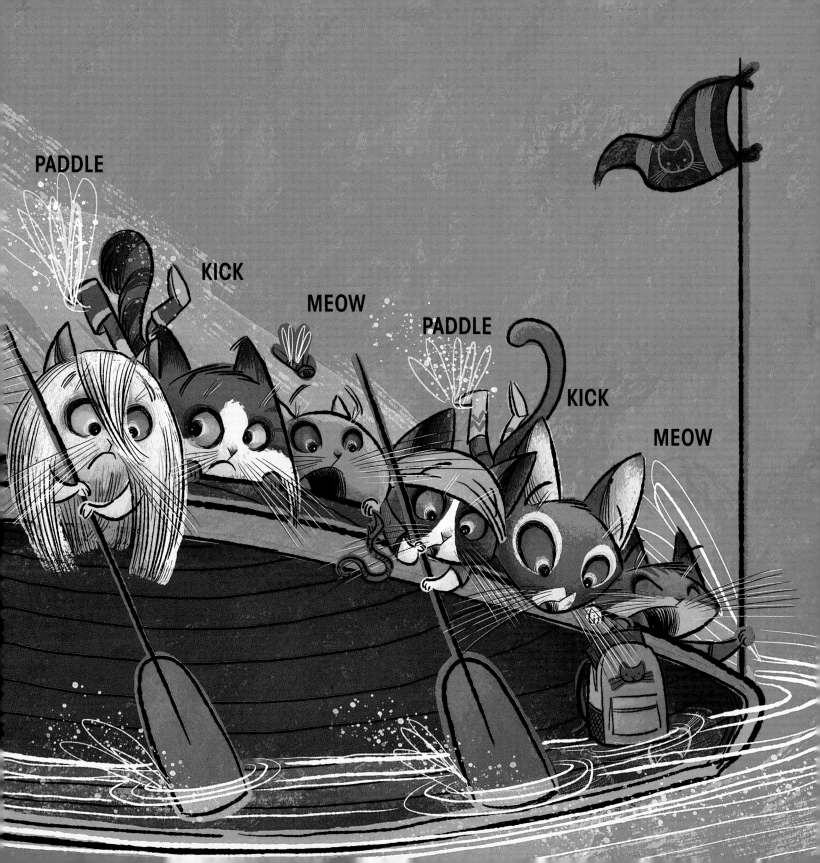

Back to camp with a

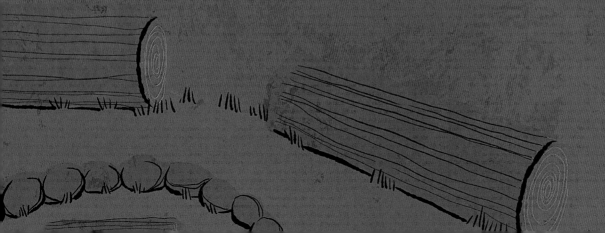

DROP

SQUISH

SQUASH

DRIP

CRUNCH!

CRUNCH?

One cat has crackers.

Captain Cat has an idea.

S'mores for dinner!

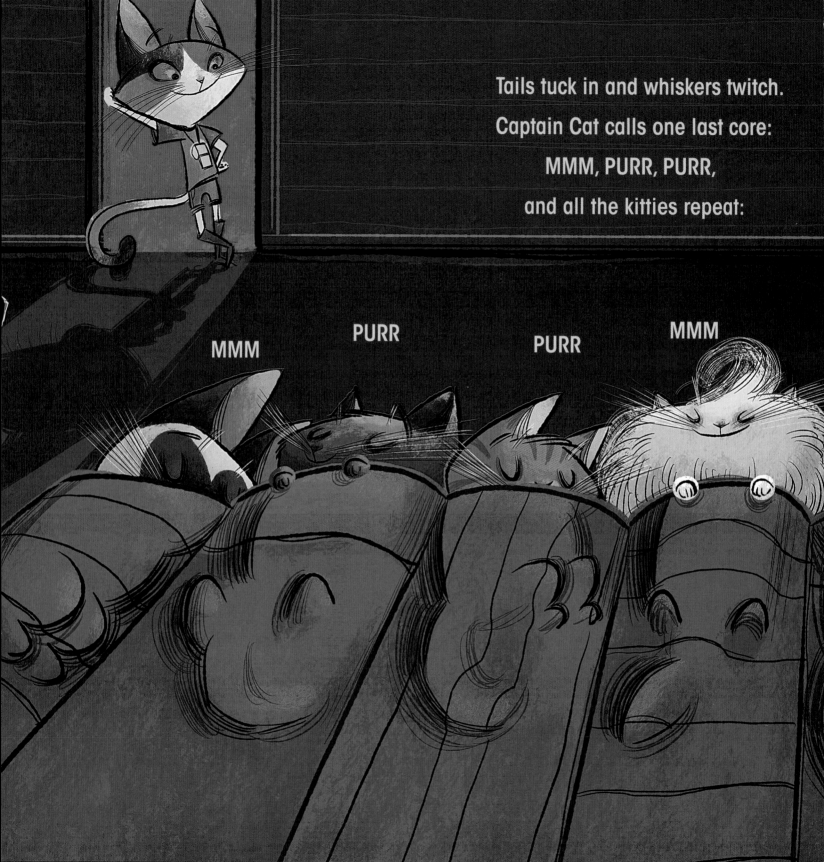

Tails tuck in and whiskers twitch.
Captain Cat calls one last core:
MMM, PURR, PURR,
and all the kitties repeat:

MMM

PURR

PURR

MMM

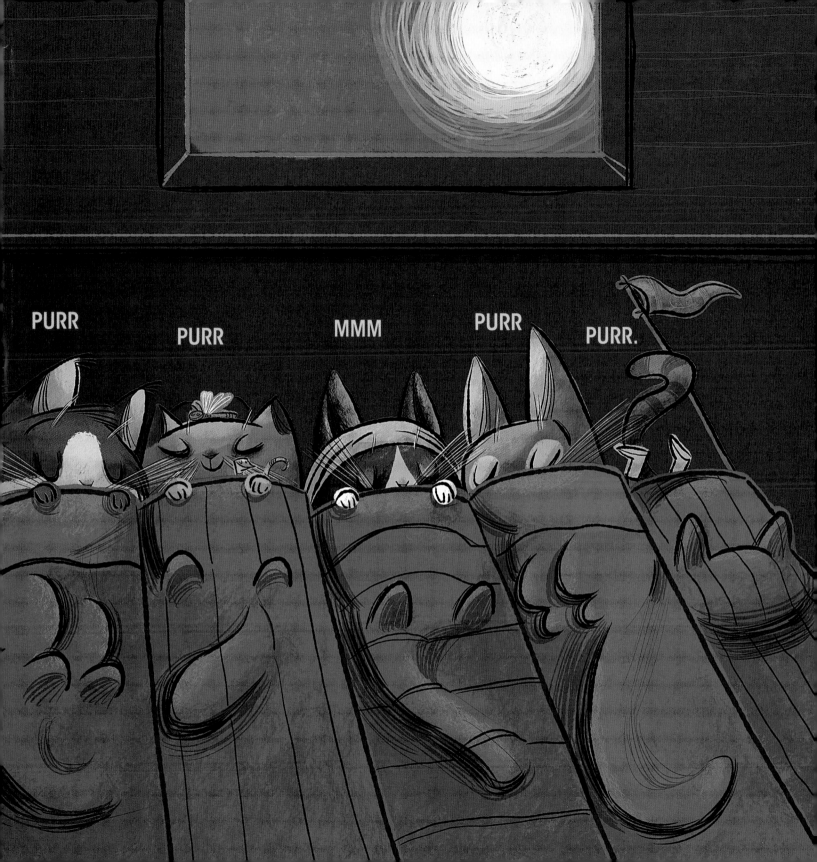

Patterns are everywhere,

and just like the cats in this book, you can make your own. You can walk one with your feet: left, right, left, right . . . You can build one with your hands: clap, clap, snap, clap, clap, snap . . . You can sing a pattern: la, di, da, la, di, da . . . If you want to make one out of objects try cereal, blocks, candy, stickers, coins, or things in nature such as sticks and pebbles.

Patterns are the foundation on which most math is built, as important as the foundation for any building. Learning to understand and recognize patterns helps you to guess or predict what will happen in math and in many areas of life. It helps you develop meaningful thinking and logic skills. When you understand patterns, you can grasp harder math problems.

But the best part about patterns is that they are so much fun, so much fun, so much fun . . .

A **repeating pattern** is a sequence that continues over and over again without changing.

A **pattern core** is the part of the pattern that keeps repeating. For example, in the pattern ABCABCABC, the pattern core is ABC.

If we transfer some of the patterns in the story to letters, here's what they would look like:

Orange, green is an AB pattern. What are the other two AB patterns in the story?

Row, row, meow is an AAB pattern. What is the other AAB pattern in the story?

Near, far, middle is an ABC pattern. What is the other ABC pattern in the story?

Drip, drop, squish, squash is an ABCD pattern. Would you make up your own ABCD pattern? You could use your voice or random objects, like this: *boop, bop, do, wop,* or sock, shoe, book, pencil.

Mmm, purr, purr is an ABB pattern. Would you make up your own ABB pattern?

Clues from Captain Cat
Did you find 14 small fish in this book? Hint: Some are swimming on the jacket and under it too! And while I tallied 172 cats, you might find more by pouncing on stray tails, ears, or paws.

For my sisters, Amy and Sara Beth,
xxo, xxo, xxo . . . —AMS

For the cast and crew of
Mad Men —JH

Text copyright © 2021 by Ann Marie Stephens
Illustrations copyright © 2021 by Jenn Harney
All rights reserved. Copying or digitizing this book for storage, display, or distribution in any other medium is strictly prohibited.

For information about permission to reproduce selections from this book, please contact permissions@bmkbooks.com.

Boyds Mills Press
An imprint of Boyds Mills & Kane,
a division of Astra Publishing House
boydsmillspress.com

Printed in China

ISBN: 978-1-63592-321-6 (hc)
ISBN: 978-1-63592-467-1 (eBook)
Library of Congress Control Number: 2020947747

First edition
10 9 8 7 6 5 4 3 2 1

Design by Barbara Grzeslo
The text is set in ITC Avant Garde Gothic.
The illustrations were created digitally.